Sally Goes to the Mountains

Written and Illustrated by

Stephen Huneck

Abrams, Books for Young Readers
New York

Acknowledgments

I wish to thank my editor Howard Reeves and his assistant Lia Ronnen for their enthusiasm and commitment to Sally's newest adventure. I also wish to thank Chantel Amey and Mike Lamp for all their help in the studio. My deepest thanks to Jim and Lynn Bryant and Will Seippel for their friendship and support. And a special thank you to my wonderful wife Gwen for her encouragement and love.

Artist's Note

One of my greatest pleasures in life is taking all of my dogs for a walk in the deep forest on my farm "Dog Mountain" in St. Johnsbury, Vermont. The dogs become super alert and never go so far that they can't keep an eye on me. Sally has a funny thing that she does—she will sit down on the trail and wait for me to miss her. As soon as I call her she comes running. She likes to know I am always thinking of her—if she only knew!

To create a woodcut print, I first draw the design of the future print in crayon, laying out the prospective shapes and colors. I then carve one block of wood for each color in the appropriate shape. The result is a series of carved blocks, one for each color in the print. After a block has been inked with its respective color, acid-free archival paper is laid onto the block and hand rubbed. I repeat the process for each color block. When this process is completed, I then hang the prints to dry. —S.H.

Designer: Ellen Nygaard Ford

The artwork for each picture is prepared with woodblock prints on paper.
The text is set in 24 point Huneck Regular.

You may visit Stephen Huneck's website at: www.huneck.com

Library of Congress Cataloging-in-Publication Data
Huneck, Stephen.
Sally goes to the mountains / written & illustrated
by Stephen Huneck.
p. cm.
Summary: Sally, a black Labrador retriever, is on her
way to go camping in the mountains.
ISBN 13: 978-0-8109-4485-5 / ISBN 10: 0-8109-4485-5
[1. Dogs—Fiction. 2. Camping—Fiction.] I. Title.
PZ7.H8995 Sal 2001
[E]—dc21 00-42153

Published in 2001 by Harry N. Abrams, Inc., New York.
All rights reserved. No part of the contents of this book may be
reproduced without the written permission of the publisher.

Printed and bound in China

10 9 8 7 6 5

HNA
harry n. abrams, inc.
a subsidiary of La Martinière Groupe
100 Fifth Avenue
New York, NY 10011
www.hnabooks.com

To dogs everywhere
and the children who love them

We are going camping in the mountains.
We read about the animals that live there.
I cannot wait to see them.

We load the van with our gear and lots of food.

"Sally, go to sleep. We will be there in the morning."

The mountains are beautiful

and hopping with life.

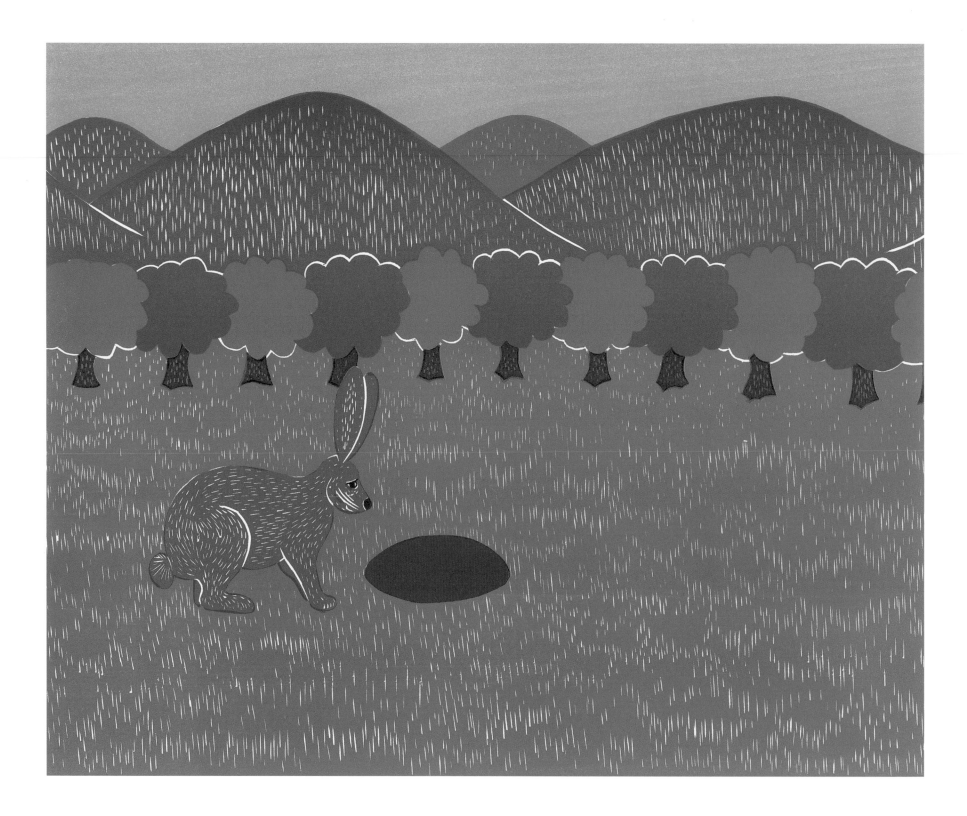

I want to play with a rabbit,

but he vanishes into thin air.

I climb a tree and meet a bird.

She sings a lovely song.

"Hi! My name is Sally." "Who?" "Sally." "Who?"

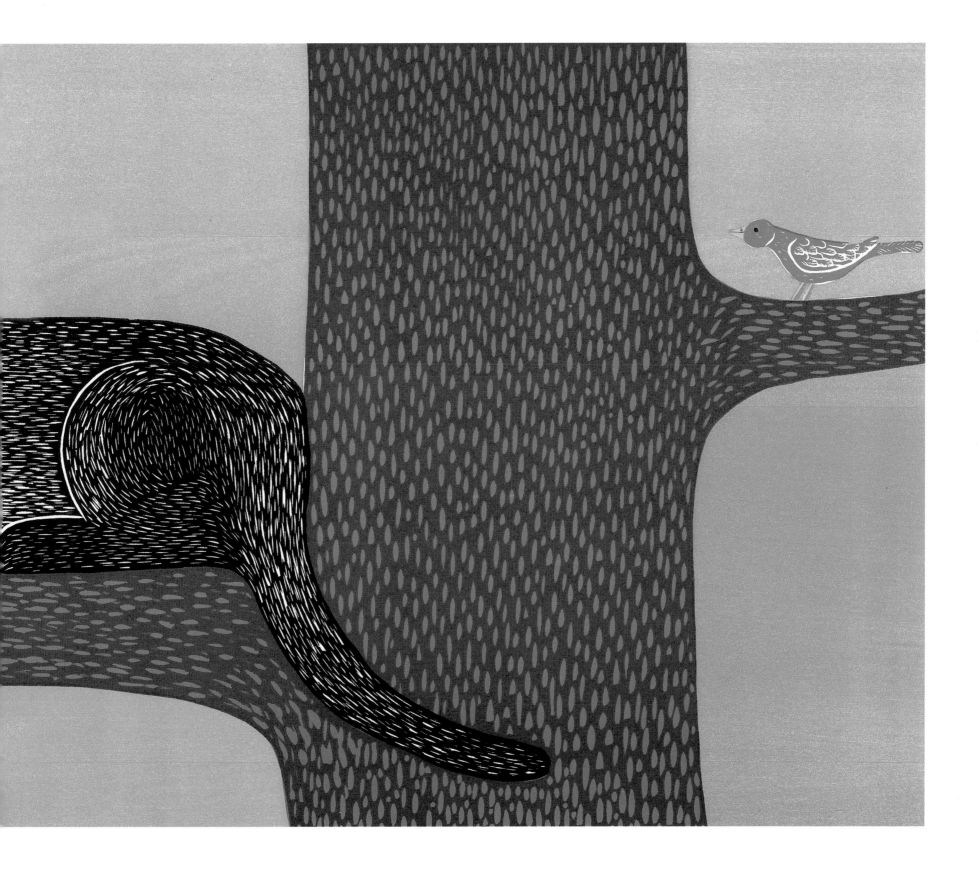

"Sally." "Who?" "Sally." "Who?" "Sally." "Who?"

I soon have enough of that.

I go for a swim.

The water is perfect,

and the fish are jumping.

I like sticks,

but the beaver has me beat.

A family of skunks is very nice,

except for one little stinker.

I want to play with a raccoon,

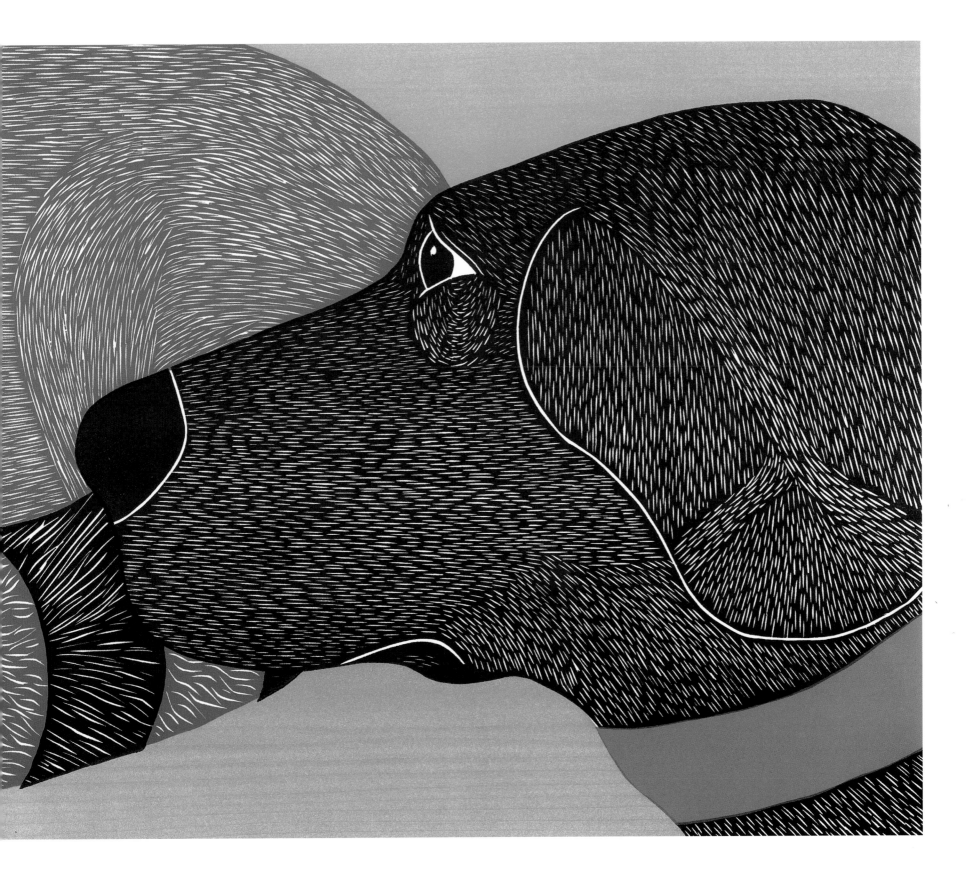

but he says, "Nighttime is playtime for me."

I see moose tracks all around . . .

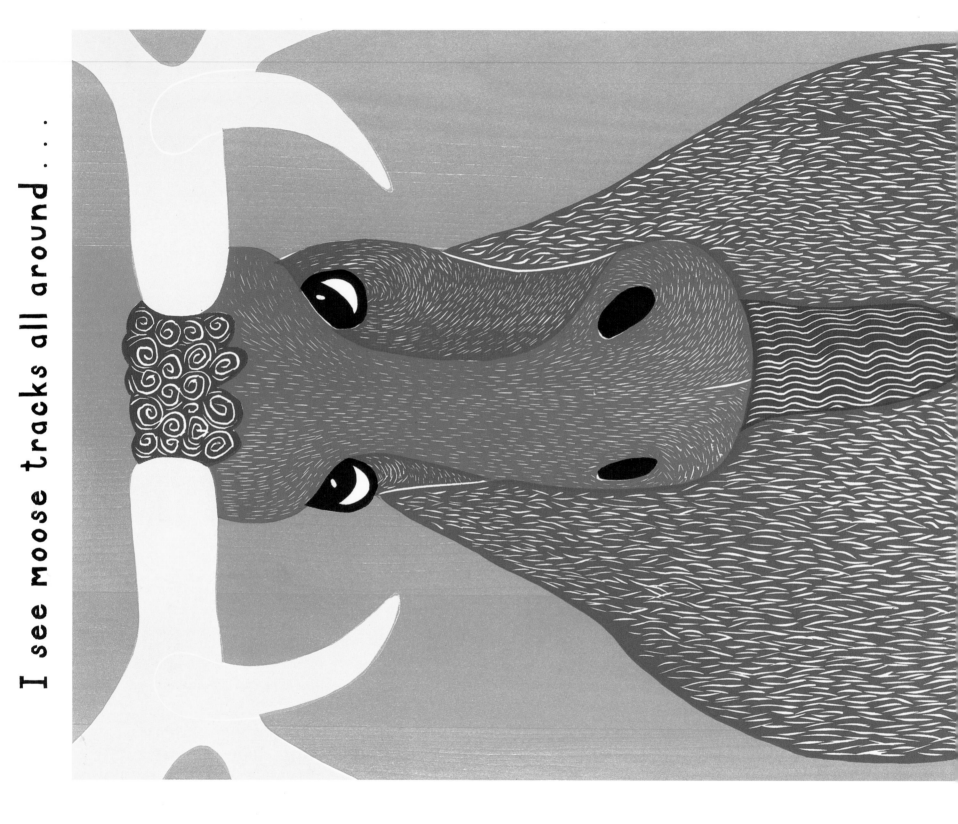

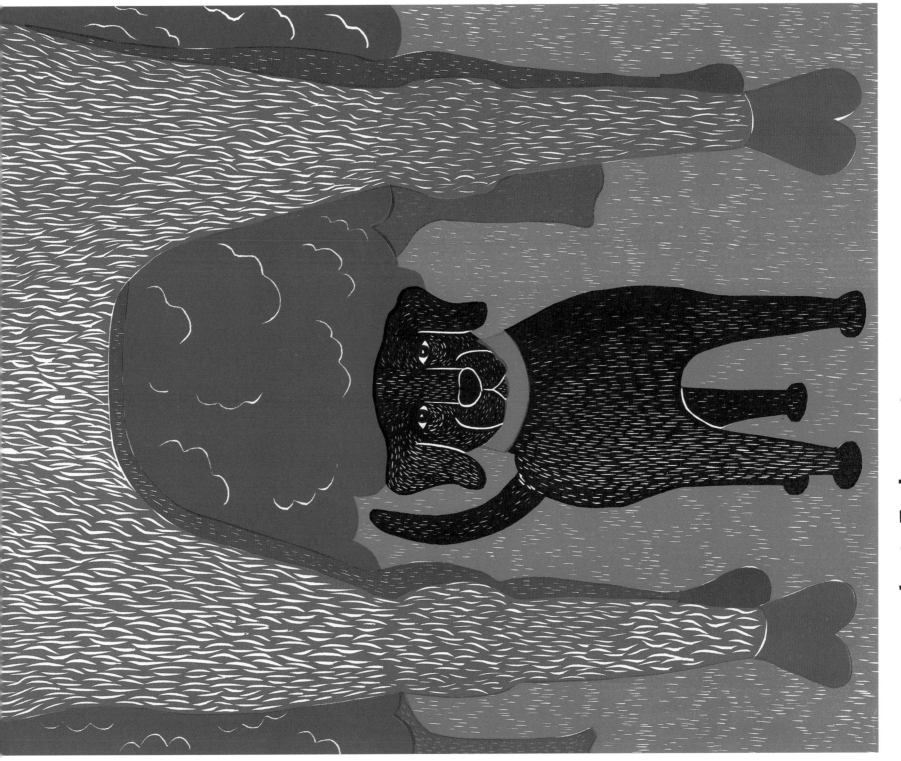

but I do not see a moose.

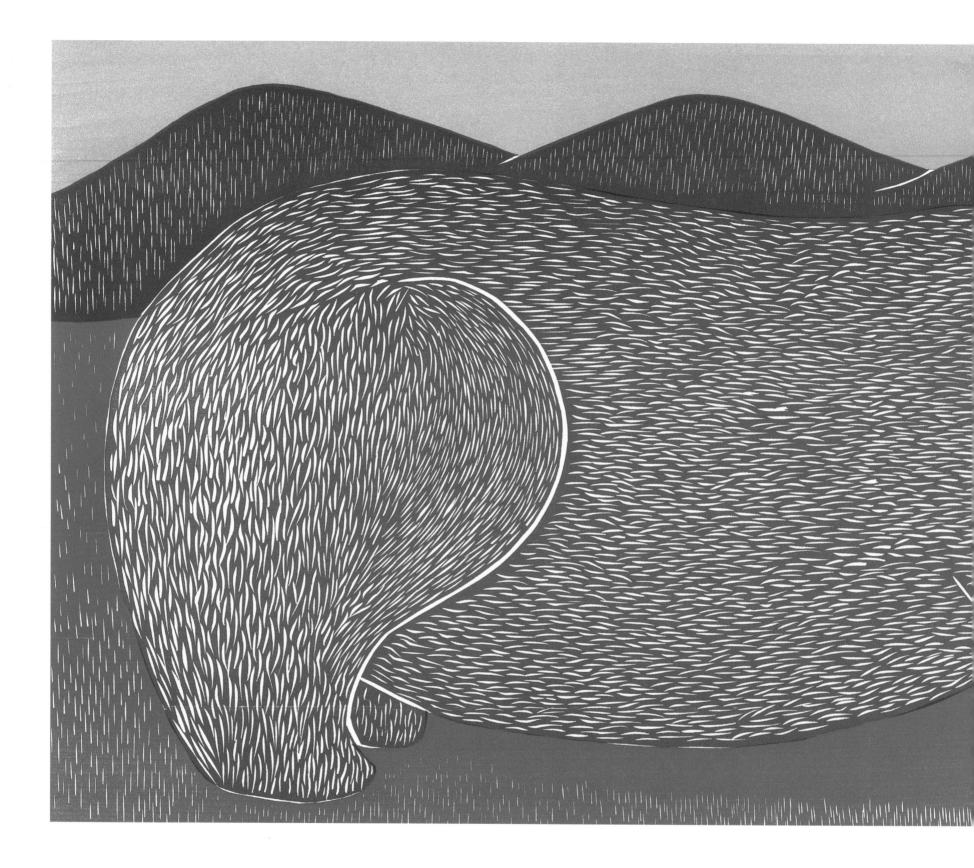

I meet a bear eating berries off a bush.

My stomach starts to growl.

I find a bush with my favorite food,
but no one to open the cans.

I have never been so hungry!

"Sally, wake up. We are in the mountains.

Time for breakfast!"

minedition

English edition published 2017 by Michael Neugebauer Publishing Ltd., Hong Kong

Text and Illustration copyright © 2017 Yoko Maruyama
Rights arranged with "minedition" Rights and Licensing AG, Zurich, Switzerland.
Michael Neugebauer Publishing Ltd.,
Unit 28, 5/F, Metro Centre, Phase 2,No.21 Lam Hing Street, Kowloon Bay, Kowloon, Hong Kong.
Phone +852 2807 1711, e-mail: info@minedition.com
This edition was printed in July 2017 at L.Rex Printing Co Ltd.
3/F., Blue Box Factory Building, 25 Hing Wo Street, Tin Wan, Aberdeen, Hong Kong, China
Typesetting in Adobe Garamond Pro
Library of Congress Cataloging-in-Publication Data available upon request.

ISBN 978-988-8341-46-7
10 9 8 7 6 5 4 3 2 1 First Impression

For more information please visit our website: www.minedition.com

minedition

No one else knows, but my dad is really Santa Claus.
We spend most of the year preparing for Christmas.
We keep reindeer in our back yard, and our house is always filled with toys.

Me last year

Having Santa for a dad is a lot of fun. But I do have one complaint.
Every Christmas Eve, when children around the world are home with their families
waiting for Santa, my dad and the reindeer fly off to deliver their presents.
Every year I have to spend Christmas Eve alone.

This year when winter came,
I wished upon the first star in the evening:
"I want to spend Christmas Eve with my father this year."

Then, the morning of Christmas Eve,
as my dad was about to prepare the sleigh,
he tripped and fell down hard.

He called a doctor, and the doctor said,
"Your ankle may be fractured. You must go to the hospital immediately."

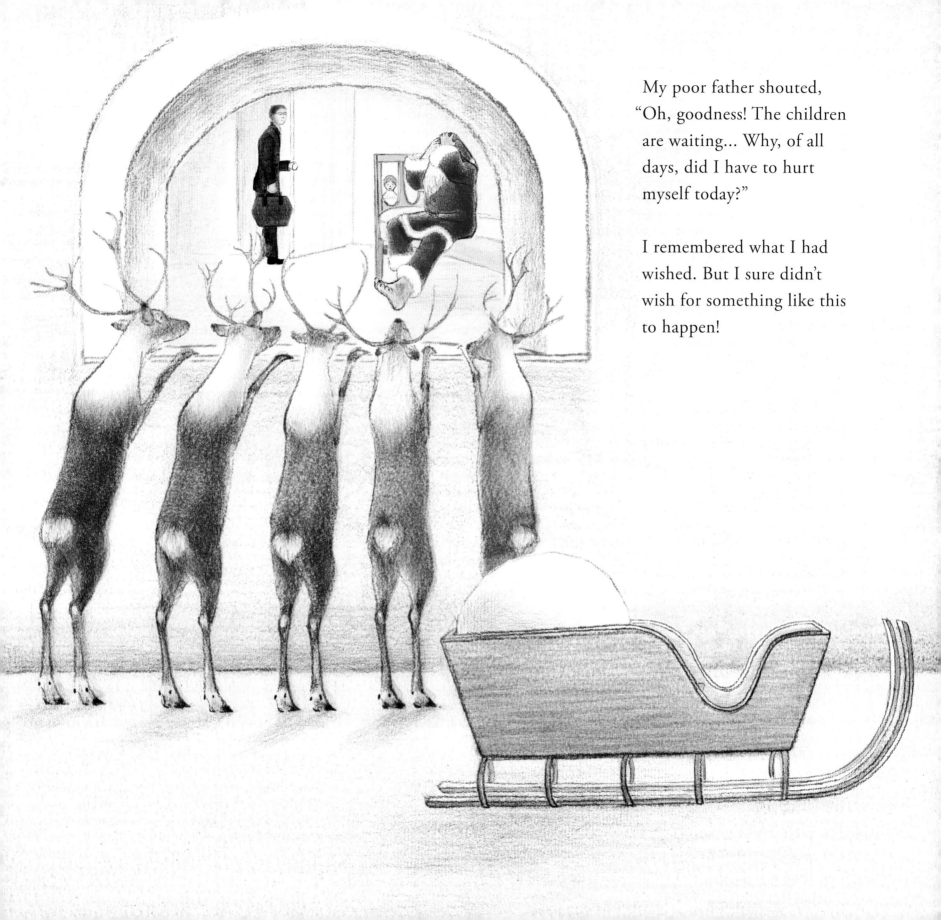

My poor father shouted,
"Oh, goodness! The children
are waiting... Why, of all
days, did I have to hurt
myself today?"

I remembered what I had
wished. But I sure didn't
wish for something like this
to happen!

My father muttered, "If only there was someone who could deliver the presents for me..."

I knew the reindeer only responded to our family,
so not just anyone could hitch them up to the sleigh.

I could only think of **one** person for the job—me!

I said,

"Maybe… if… perhaps… I could deliver the presents…?"

Dad's face lit up.

"Yes!" he exclaimed with delight.

"Of course, you can do it!"

I rushed to put on my dad's red coat and hat.
No one makes Santa clothes in my size,
so my outfit looked pretty silly.

My dad told me, "It isn't Santa's appearance
that's the important thing.
The most important thing is..."

"What's in your heart," I finished.

Dad smiled.

Finally I was ready to go.

The presents were loaded, and the reindeer were eager to get started.

I stepped into the sleigh and pulled on the reins, and I before I knew it we zoomed away into the sky!

I waved back at my dad and Rudolph,
the one reindeer we'd left behind to keep him company.

Flying the sleigh took some getting used to.
It swayed from side to side in the wind, and sometimes
it lurched so hard that I felt like I might fall out.

Eventually I got the hang of it, grasping the reins with more confidence.
Before long we had zipped over valleys, over forests, and crossed the pitch-black sea.

After a while, the air gradually became warmer, and the smell of the air changed.
The reindeer knew right where to change course.
I saw a small town's lights approaching in the distance,
and I felt so excited to be doing Santa's work
for the very first time.

We visited many houses, and I delivered a lot of presents.
At first I had plenty of energy, but as the night wore on I got more and more tired.
I started to realize what a tough job my dad has.
Sweaty and panting, I somehow managed to deliver every last present.

But then, just as I thought we were leaving, the reindeer made a turn toward
the forest and landed on the roof of a small, shabby house—
even though there were no more presents left in my sack.

I wondered if there was some mistake,
but they nudged me toward the chimney,
so I climbed down.

When I entered the house I saw no
Christmas decorations anywhere,
and there was little food in the kitchen.
It didn't feel at all like Christmas Eve.
I peeked into the bedroom where a girl
was sleeping. I noticed there were
worn-out ballerina shoes beside her bed,
and I found a letter in the stocking by
the foot of her bed. Carefully I opened
the letter and read it.

"Dear Santa Claus,
Yesterday in my dream I became a snow
fairy and danced in the ballet. I wish you
would make it snow for me on Christmas.
                              Love, Sara."

This was one gift I couldn't deliver.

Suddenly I heard the sound of hooves outside.

Clip-clop, clip-clop, clip-clop.

I spun around and saw a large shadow appear in the window.

My heart skipped a beat.

But what was this?

It was my dad!

"I'm glad I caught you,"
he said cheerfully.
"It looks like you've done a great job.
Why do you look so down?"

I showed the letter to my father.
"I can't make this wish come true," I said.

"Well," Dad said,
"I was able to bring one last special gift."
He pointed to another enormous sack he had
brought outside the window.

"I brought a little bit of the North Pole here," Dad said, opening the sack.
A huge cloud floated out and rose up slowly over the town.
Shortly after, snow started to fall!

Then my dad winked at me and said,
"Now all the gifts have been delivered.
Let's go home."

On the ride home I said,
"That must have been the world's biggest gift!"

Dad said, "No, her biggest, best gift is something
I could never deliver. It's something she has already."

"What do you mean?" I asked.

Dad said,
"The word 'gift' has two meanings.
It can be a 'present,' sure.
But a gift can also be a 'talent.'
Some gifts wear out after a year or two,
but the gift Sara has is limitless,
and it will last her a lifetime."

I thought about that for a while.

Then my dad asked me,
"By the way,
what gift did you wish for this year?"

I just smiled.
My wish had come true already.